Harry Gets an Uncle

by BARBARA ANN PORTE

pictures by
YOSSI ABOLAFIA

Greenwillow Books
NEW YORK

*Watercolor paints and a black pen were
used for the full-color art.
The text type is Plantin.*

*Printed in Hong Kong by
South China Printing Company (1988) Ltd.
First Edition   10 9 8 7 6 5 4 3 2 1*

*Library of Congress Cataloging-in-Publication Data
Porte, Barbara Ann.
Harry gets an uncle / by Barbara Ann Porte;
pictures by Yossi Abolafia.
p.   cm.
Summary: Harry is worried about being the ring
boy at his Aunt Rose's wedding, after he hears
his friend Dorcas tell horror stories about
what went wrong at her Uncle Fred's wedding.
ISBN 0-688-09389-2 (trade). ISBN 0-688-09390-6 (lib.)
[1. Weddings—Fiction.]   I. Abolafia, Yossi, ill.
II. Title.
PZ7.P7995Han   1991   [E]—dc20
90-39562   CIP   AC*

I, Harry, am going to a wedding.

"I'm getting married, Harry,"
my Aunt Rose said.

"Mr. Baxter will be your Uncle Leo."

"Congratulations," I said.

"I've never had an uncle before."

Aunt Rose and I have known
Mr. Baxter for a long time.
He plays the tuba in "Red Rose Quintet,"
Aunt Rose's five-piece band.
Aunt Rose sings and plays piano.

I tell my friend Dorcas the news.

"I've never been to a wedding," I say.

"Really?" she says.

"I went to a wedding once.

My Uncle Fred got married.

It was awful."

"Awful how?" I ask her.

Dorcas tells me.

"There were a zillion relatives,"
she says. "Most of them
I'd never seen before.
They pinched my cheeks and said,
'Isn't she sweet? My, how she's grown!'
I was the flower girl.
My dress was long and hot and prickly.
It tripped me whenever I walked.
The flowers were roses,
with thorns that stuck me.
Losing the ring was the worst part."

"You lost the ring?" I ask.

"It was my brother Billy's fault,"
  Dorcas says.

"Carrying the ring was his job,
  but he came down with chicken pox.
  'You're next in line,'
  my Uncle Fred told me.
  'But I'm the flower girl,' I said.
  'Dorcas will be glad to do both,'
  my mother told him.

"I walked down the aisle carefully,
holding the roses in one hand
and the wedding band,
on a velvet pillow, in the other.

"Just as I got to the altar,
  the pillow tilted.
  The ring slipped off it,
  rolled under a table,
  and stuck in a crack in the floor.

"The entire wedding party
    wound up on their hands and knees
    underneath the table,
    looking for the ring.
    After they found it,
    they couldn't get it up.

"Uncle Fred borrowed my mother's ring
and married Aunt Esther with it.
After the ceremony,
they moved the table
and pried up the ring with a fork.
It's still a little bent.
Believe me, Aunt Esther wasn't pleased.

"The next week,
   while she and Uncle Fred
   were on their honeymoon,
   I was home in bed
   with chicken pox."

"I think I'll skip Aunt Rose's wedding,"
I tell my father that night,
"and stay at home with Girl."
(Girl is my dog.
She lives with my Aunt Rose
because my father is allergic,
but she's spending
their honeymoon with us.)

"Skip?" my father says.

"You're Aunt Rose's ring boy."

"No one told me that," I tell him.

"I just did, right now," he says.

"Anyway, if you stay home,
you'll be at the wedding.
Aunt Rose is getting married here,
in our backyard."

"How will everybody fit?" I ask.

"Everybody who?" my father says.

I tell him what Dorcas told me.

"When her Uncle Fred got married,
a zillion people came."

"So far as I know," my father says,
"the only people coming here
    are a few close relatives and friends."
"Yes, but what about the ring?" I ask.
    I tell him what happened to Dorcas.
    My father sighs.
"Please, Harry," he says.
"Believe me, such a thing
    won't happen twice."

Right, I think, but something else
could happen, even worse.

"Your aunt could move away
and take Girl with her,"
Dorcas says when I tell her.
"That would be worse."
"Why would she want to do that?"
I ask.
"Most people move away
after they get married,"
Dorcas explains.

"My Uncle Fred, for instance,
lived next door to us
until he got married.
Then Aunt Esther saw an ad
in the paper.
'Circus Help Wanted,' it read.
'I've always wanted to be
in the circus,' she said.
It turned out, so had Uncle Fred.
They both got jobs selling tickets.
Now Aunt Esther's a clown.
Uncle Fred feeds the elephants
and hoses them down.
The only time we see them
is when the circus comes to town."

After school, I visit my Aunt Rose.

"Hi, Harry," she says.

"I'm glad you're here.

I can use a hand with the dusting."

We start on her piano.

Girl puts her front paws

on the bench and watches.

"What's on your mind, Harry?"

Aunt Rose asks.

"You look a little worried."

"Who, me?" I answer.

Girl yawns.

"I think Girl's worried

about where she'll live

when you move away,"

I tell Aunt Rose.

Aunt Rose looks surprised.

"I'm not moving anyplace," she says.

I tell her what Dorcas told me.

"I see," says Aunt Rose.

"*Some* people move after they get married.

Uncle Leo, for instance.

When we get back

from our honeymoon in Bermuda,

he's moving in here."

I'm glad to hear it.

That's when I bring up the ring.

"I've decided to carry it in my pocket,"

I tell Aunt Rose.

"I think that way,

I probably won't drop it."

Aunt Rose smiles.

"Don't worry," she says.

"I'm sure you won't.

I only hope it doesn't rain.

That would be awful."

Yes, I think.

The guests would get wet.

The cake would be ruined.

Fortunately, Aunt Rose's wedding day
is sunny. Benches have been put
in the yard. The cake and food

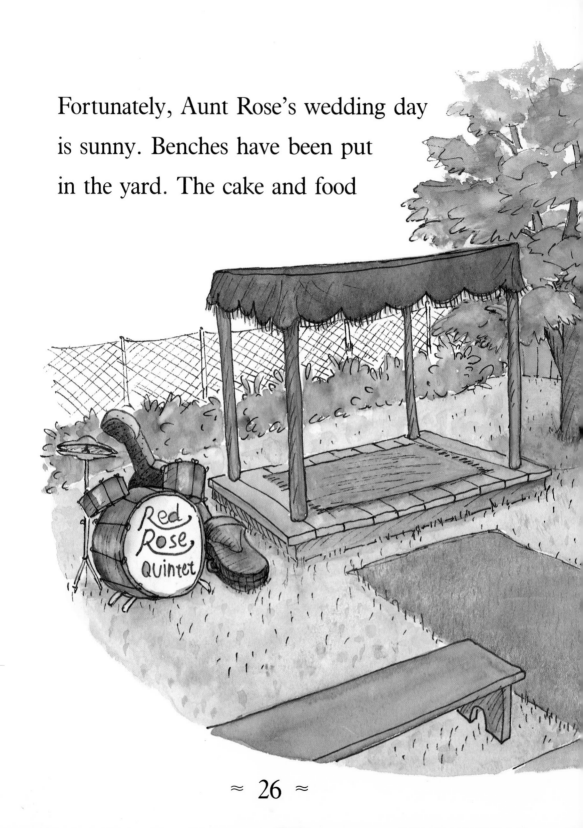

have been set out on long tables.
Beside the dogwood tree,
there is a canopy.
They will be married underneath it.

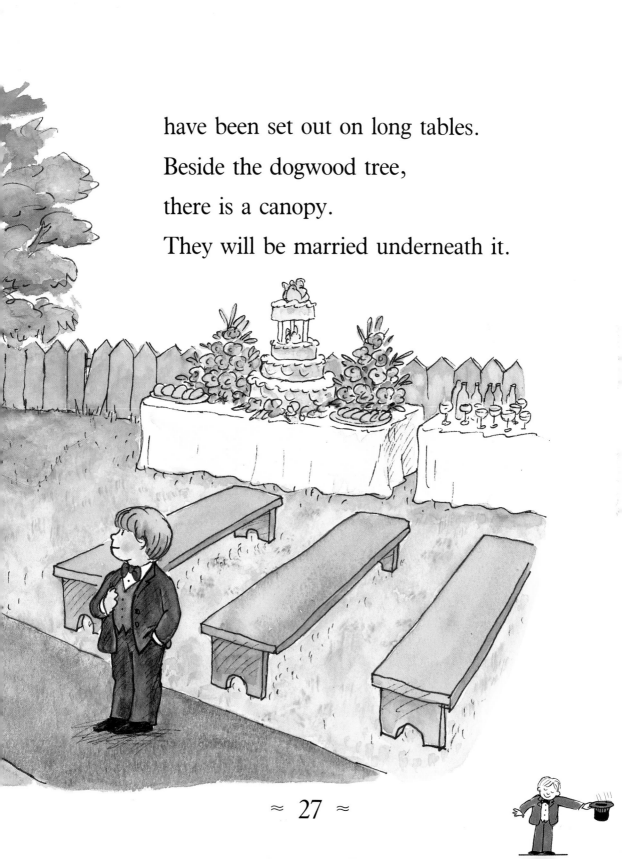

Girl is safely inside the house
when the guests begin arriving.
"My, how Harry has grown,"
a few of them say.
So far, no one has pinched my cheek.

The musicians from Aunt Rose's band
are here: Luke, on bass;
the drummer, Lucille;
and Herbert, who plays French horn.
The music begins.
I put my hand in my pocket
to be sure the ring is still there.
I hold onto it tightly.

Uncle Leo's niece, Denise,
walks down the aisle first,
holding the flowers. I go next.

After me come the bridesmaids and ushers,
and then Uncle Leo and my father,
who is best man.

The band swings into
"Here Comes the Bride."
Aunt Rose starts down the aisle,
holding onto Grandpa's arm.
She is dressed all in white,
with a train and a veil.
Aunt Rose looks beautiful.

The guests all smile.

Then some of them begin to giggle.

I see why.

Girl is walking down the aisle,

right behind Aunt Rose and Grandpa.

I wonder how she got out of the house.

When Aunt Rose and Grandpa
stop beside Uncle Leo,
Girl keeps going.
She sits in the shade
of the dogwood tree
and watches the ceremony.

Part way through it, just as I am about
to hand Uncle Leo the ring,
Ms. Parker's cat, Tulip,
who lives next door,
squeezes through the fence
to see what's going on.

Girl sees her, barks, and runs over.

Tulip sees Girl.

She puts up her back and hisses.

Then she dashes for the dogwood tree,

with Girl at her heels.

Tulip races up the tree trunk.
She stretches out on a high branch
and looks down.
Girl sits at the foot of the tree
and looks up.

The wedding has come to a standstill.

No one seems to know what to do.

Uncle Leo clears his throat.

"Harry," he says. "If you have the ring, I think the wedding can proceed."

I hand him the ring.

He winks at me.

He doesn't look even a little angry.

He puts the ring on Aunt Rose's finger
and kisses her. The band begins to play.

I take Girl inside the house.

Ms. Parker comes over from next door
and coaxes Tulip down from the tree.
"I'm so sorry about the disturbance,"
she says to Aunt Rose.
"It was a lovely wedding, anyway,
and you are a beautiful bride."

Then, holding onto Tulip with one hand, she reaches out with the other and pinches Aunt Rose's cheek.

All the guests are eating and talking
and dancing.

Aunt Rose and I, Uncle Leo
and my father, Denise and her parents
join hands and dance together
in a circle.

When the wedding is over
and the guests have gone home,
Uncle Leo gives me a wristwatch.
"It's to thank you," he says,
"for being such a good ring boy and nephew."
"Thank you," I tell him.

"How was the wedding?"

Dorcas asks the next day

when I show her my wristwatch.

"Fine," I say.

"I didn't drop the ring.

Ms. Parker's cat caused a disturbance,

but other than that,

nothing bad happened.

We all had a very good time.

Even Girl did."

A few days later, a postcard
arrives from Bermuda.
On one side is a picture
of Aunt Rose and Uncle Leo, waving.
On the other side, it says,

"We're having a wonderful time.

We miss you all.

Give Girl a pat for us.

Love, Aunt Rose and Uncle Leo."

BARBARA ANN PORTE's stories and poems for adults have appeared in literary magazines in the United States and Canada. She is the author of *I Only Made Up the Roses*, *The Kidnapping of Aunt Elizabeth*, *Jesse's Ghost and Other Stories* and, for younger readers, the <u>Harry</u> books: *Harry's Visit*, *Harry's Dog*, *Harry in Trouble* (all three, ALA Notable books), and *Harry's Mom*.

YOSSI ABOLAFIA was born in Israel. He is the author-artist of *Fox Tale*, *My Three Uncles*, *Yanosh's Island*, and *A Fish for Mrs. Gardenia*. Among the many books he has illustrated are *It's Valentine's Day* and *My Parents Think I'm Sleeping*, both by Jack Prelutsky; Barbara Ann Porte's <u>Harry</u> books; and *Leo and Emily's Zoo* by Franz Brandenberg. He lives with his wife and three children near Jerusalem.

JE
Porte, Barbara Ann.
Harry gets an uncle
$13.95